THIS WALKER BOOK BELONGS TO:

_____

_____

_____

_____

For Caz

First published 1996 by Walker Books Ltd
87 Vauxhall Walk, London SE11 5HJ

This edition published 1997

2 4 6 8 10 9 7 5 3 1

© 1996 Clara Vulliamy

This book has been typeset in Ehrhardt.

Printed in Hong Kong

British Library Cataloguing in Publication Data
A catalogue record for this book is
available from the British Library.

ISBN 0-7445-5252-4

ELLEN
AND
PENGUIN
AND THE NEW BABY

CLARA VULLIAMY

WALKER BOOKS
AND SUBSIDIARIES
LONDON • BOSTON • SYDNEY

Ellen had a new baby brother.

Penguin wasn't sure if he liked
new baby brothers much.

Everywhere Ellen and Penguin went,

the baby came too.

When they wanted a quiet story,
the baby started crying.

And because Mum
was too busy to
help them,

a lot went
wrong.

The baby was given Ellen's old mobile
with the woolly sheep hanging down.

"Penguin's cross," said Ellen.

"He likes that mobile."

Ellen and Penguin got into the baby's
carrycot and pretended it was a little boat
taking them far away to sea.

"You'd better get out
or you'll break it," said Mum.

In the night,
Penguin
couldn't
sleep.

So Ellen had to bring him downstairs
and walk round and round with him,
patting his back.

The next morning everyone was tired.
Mum said, "What we need is a nice day
out. Where shall we go?" Ellen chose
the park with the farm animals.

Ellen and Penguin were so
excited they ran all the
way down the path to
where the animals lived.

They saw some lambs and
a family of little startled chicks.

Penguin's favourites were the
snuffly piglets with curly tails.

Ellen liked the baby rabbits,
snuggling together in the grass.

While Mum was unpacking the lunch,
the baby started crying again.
"Could you try and cheer him up?" said Mum.

Penguin wasn't sure what
to do, but Ellen said,
"Poor baby."

They tried a rattle
from his bag,

and a bear
and a book,
but he went
on crying.

Then Penguin did a little dance.

The baby stopped crying and looked.

Ellen and Penguin danced
round and round and got
more and more dizzy.

They collapsed in a
heap, laughing.

And the baby joined in.
"Our baby loves us," said Ellen.
And they both agreed that new baby
brothers weren't so bad after all.

MORE WALKER PAPERBACKS
For You to Enjoy

ELLEN AND PENGUIN
by Clara Vulliamy

Ellen is small and shy. So is her soft-toy penguin. But, as they discover
at the park, they are not the only ones.

"This is a delightful story which should help anxious and emotionally
insecure children to feel less isolated." *Child Education*

0-7445-3658-8   £4.50

DANNY'S DUCK
by June Crebbin/Clara Vulliamy

Danny makes a secret discovery at the edge of the
school playground: a nesting duck.

"Simple and charming… Vulliamy's drawings endear us to Danny
and duck alike." *The Observer*

0-7445-4371-1   £4.99

ZA-ZA'S BABY BROTHER
by Lucy Cousins

Life is not the same when your mum has a new baby, as young zebra
Za-za discovers in this enchanting story by the creator of the Maisy books.

"A delightful book." *The School Librarian*

0-7445-4764-4   £5.99